Mama, Daddy, Baby and Me

story by
Lisa Gewing

drawings by
Donna Larimer

SPIRIT PRESS
Santa Cruz

for Sasha and Nicky

Copyright © 1989 by Lisa Gewing.
Illustrations © 1989 by Donna Larimer.
All rights reserved.

Published in the United States by Spirit Press, 1005 Granite Ridge Drive, Santa Cruz, CA 95065
Distributed by Publishers Group West, 4065 Hollis, Emeryville, CA 94608. Printed in Hong Kong.

3rd printing, 1991

Library of Congress Cataloging in Publication Data

Gewing, Lisa, 1933-
   Mama, Daddy, Baby, and Me/by Gewing;
   Illustrated by Donna Larimer
   Summary: Presents a small child's perception of Mother's pregnancy,
   the family's preparations for the birth, and the arrival of the new baby.
   ISBN 0-944296-04-01 : $12.95
   (1. Babies—Fiction.) I. Larimer, Donna, 1945-   ill.
   II. Title.
   PZ7.G335Mam 1989
(E)—dc19

88-35483
CIP-AC

Mama's tummy is big and round.

Baby is inside.

Once I lived in Mama's tummy.

Then I came outside.

This was my little bed.

This was my swing.

See my tiny socks,
my shirts,
and other baby things?

Baby needs diapers

and blankets

and here's a little hat.

Mama's getting ready and I help her pack.

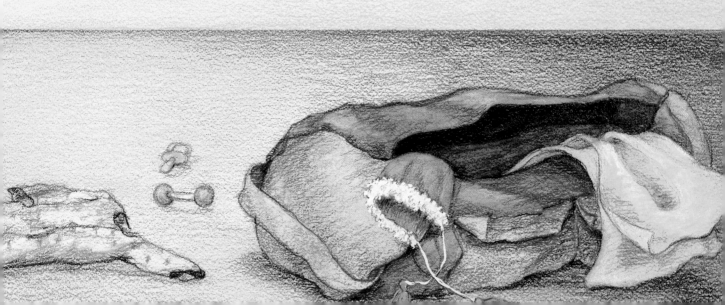

When baby is ready Mama knows.

Away to the hospital

with Daddy she goes.

Grandma comes and stays with me.

We have lots of fun.

She reads me stories

and we play hide and run.

Mama and Daddy
are home again.

They hug me
and I hug them.

Here is the Baby.

Shh, Baby's asleep.

Hear Baby crying?

See Baby eat?

Baby is so very small.

Baby can't do much at all.

I am big. I laugh and play.

"I am a helper,"

Mama and Daddy say.

I bring Baby's diapers.

I shake Baby's keys.

Here's a hug for Baby.

Here's a hug for me.

There's lots of love
for both of us.

This is my family.